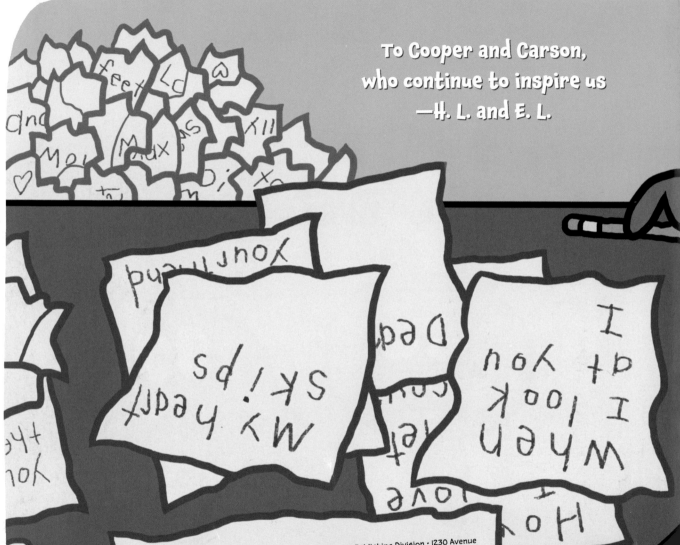

To Cooper and Carson,
who continue to inspire us
—H. L. and E. L.

ALADDIN · An imprint of Simon & Schuster Children's Publishing Division · 1230 Avenue of the Americas, New York, NY 10020 · First Aladdin hardcover edition December 2013 · Text copyright © 2013 by Heather Long · Illustrations copyright © 2013 by Ethan Long · All rights reserved, including the right of reproduction in whole or in part in any form. · ALADDIN is a trademark of Simon & Schuster, Inc., and related logo is a registered trademark of Simon & Schuster, Inc. · For information about special discounts for bulk purchases, please contact Simon & Schuster Special Sales at 1-866-506-1949 or business@simonandschuster.com. · The Simon & Schuster Speakers Bureau can bring authors to your live event. For more information or to book an event contact the Simon & Schuster Speakers Bureau at 1-866-248-3049 or visit our website at www.simonspeakers.com. · Designed by Jessica Handelman · The text of this book was set in Chaloops Medium and

You Smell like a rose

ChaloopsDecaf. · The illustrations for this book were rendered digitally. · Manufactured in China 0913 SCP · 2 4 6 8 10 9 7 5 3 1 · Library of Congress Cataloging-in-Publication Data: Long, Heather. The mixed-up message / by Heather & Ethan Long. — First Aladdin hardcover edition. pages cm. — (Max & Milo) Summary: Younger beaver brother Milo is determined to help his older brother Max win the affections of Molly, whether Max likes it or not. ISBN 978-1-4424-5140-7 (hardcover) — ISBN 978-1-4424-5142-1 (ebook) [1. Brothers–Fiction. 2. Beavers–Fiction. 3. Humorous stories.] I. Long, Ethan, illustrator. II. Title. PZ7.L8466Mix 2013 [E]–dc23
2012045683

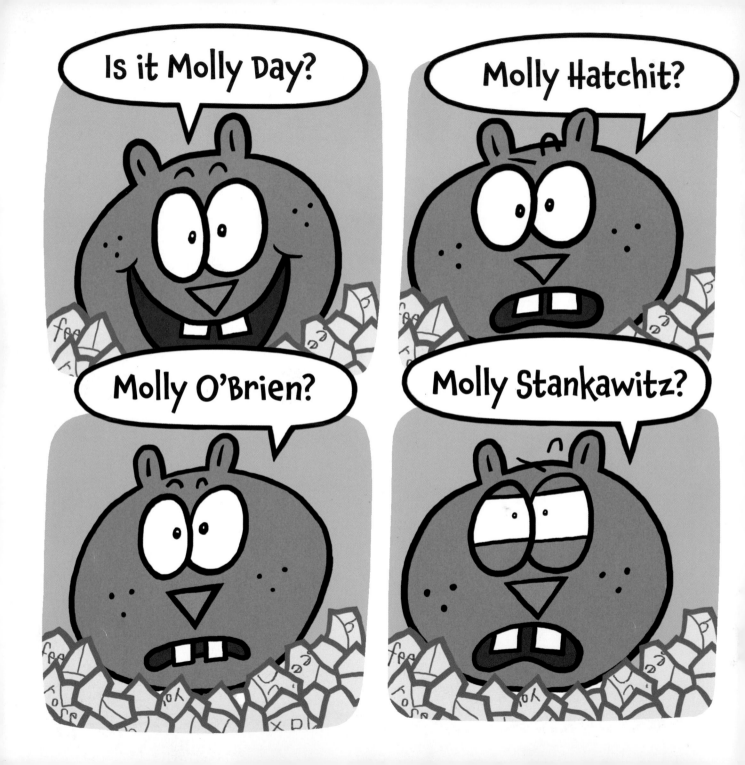

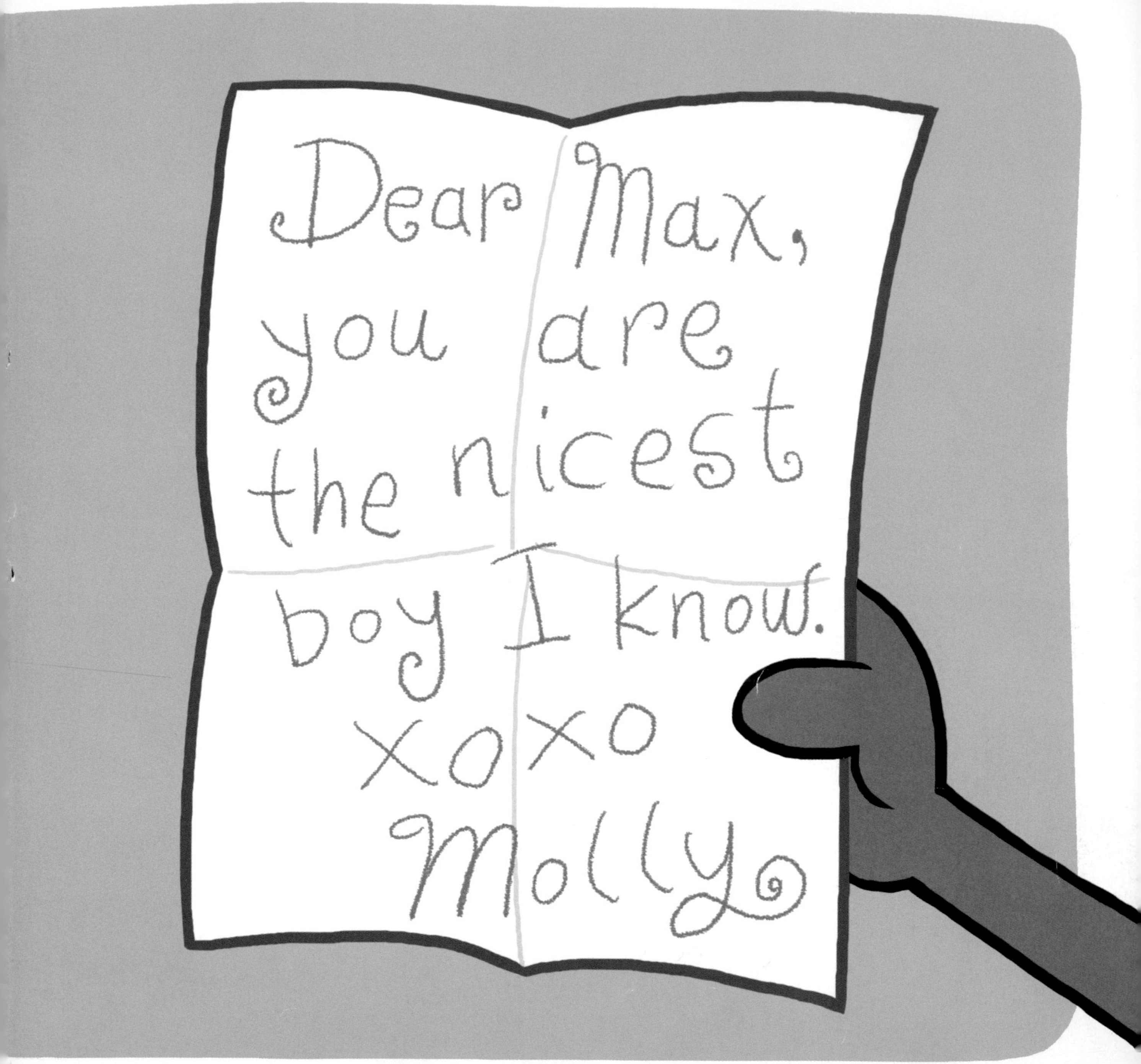
Dear Max,
you are
the nicest
boy I know.
xoxo
Molly